Praise for the ~~...~~ les:

"Max and Sid … have undeniable chemistry … Wiebe takes her time
with the snappy, fleet dialog, making it more than a means of keeping
the reader up to speed …" – *The Horn Book*

"Max's hilarious get-rich-quick schemes make an entertaining read for kids
discovering chapter books for the first time …" – *Canadian Bookseller*

"The mystery element will appeal to crime-solving readers …
Max and Sid are quirky and likable characters whose daring exploits
reveal cleverness and spunk." – *Children's Literature*

"… engaging and lively …" – *Midwest Book Review*

"… just the right amount of humour and mystery."

Now

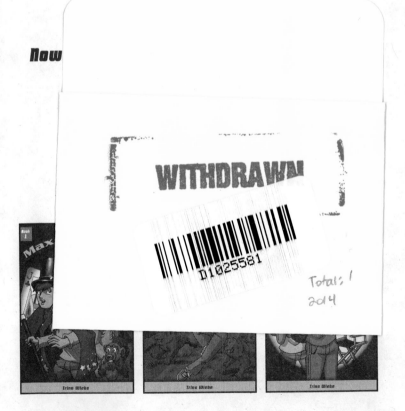

Max the Businessman

by **Trina Wiebe**

Illustrations by David Okum

Lobster Press ™

Max the Businessman
Text © 2008 Trina Wiebe
Illustrations © 2008 David Okum

Published in 2008 by Lobster Press™
1620 Sherbrooke Street West, Suites C & D
Montréal, Québec   H3H 1C9
Tel. (514) 904-1100 • Fax (514) 904-1101 • www.lobsterpress.com

Publisher: Alison Fripp
Editor: Meghan Nolan
Editorial Assistant: Emma Stephen
Graphic Design & Production: Tammy Desnoyers

We acknowledge the financial support of the Government of Canada through the
Book Publishing Industry Development Program (BPIDP) for our publishing activities.

We acknowledge the support of the Canada
Council for the Arts for our publishing program.

The Canada Council | Le Conseil des Arts
for the Arts | du Canada

Library and Archives Canada Cataloguing in Publication

Wiebe, Trina, 1970-
    Max the businessman / by Trina Wiebe ; illustrations by David Okum.

(Max-a-million, ISSN 1701-4557 ; 4)
ISBN 978-1-897073-93-3

    I. Okum, David, 1967- II. Title. III. Series: Wiebe, Trina, 1970-
Max-a-million ; 4.

PS8595.I358M394 2008   jC813'.6   C2008-901091-4

Printed and bound in Canada.

Text is printed on Rolland Enviro 100 Book,
100% recycled post-consumer fibre.

Table of Contents

1 The Big Cheese

"I'm bored," moaned Max. He leaned against the glass counter of the Vegetarian Deli and plucked an organic gelatin-free gumdrop out of a glass jar. He popped it into his mouth, chewed twice, then swallowed. "There's nothing to do in this town during summer vacation."

Sid eyed the half-empty jar. "*Blech.* Those things are full of vitamins." Her parents, who owned the store, only sold healthy treats. Sid loved candy almost as much as she loved baseball, so she kept a stash of the good stuff at Max's house to avoid a lecture.

Max shrugged. "They're not so bad. And like I said, I'm bored."

"I'm almost done with my shift," said Sid. "Want to go to the pool?"

Max frowned. "No."

"Mini golf?" suggested Sid.

Max shook his head.

"The movies?" tried Sid. "Go-carts? Bowling?"

"I can't," wailed Max. He pulled a handful of coins out of his pocket and spread them on the countertop. "I've got exactly three dollars and seventeen cents," he said, staring at the money glumly. "That's not enough to rent one smelly bowling shoe, let alone play a whole game."

"Ask your dad for an advance on your allowance," said Sid.

"This *is* an advance on my allowance!" Max sighed and reached for another gumdrop. "I don't have enough money to do anything fun. If only I ..."

"Was a famous magician or a superhero or a movie director," Sid finished his sentence for him. "You know, sometimes I wish you'd just hurry up and win the lottery already. Getting rich is all you

ever talk about."

"That's not true," protested Max. He thought about it for a moment, then shrugged. Maybe Sid had a point. Max did think about money an awful lot. With a couple million dollars in his pocket he could buy every computer game ever invented, travel around the world a dozen times, and still have enough left over to cure a few diseases. Heck, maybe he'd even give his parents an allowance!

He wasn't greedy, really. It just seemed logical that since he had a ritzy-sounding name like Maxamillian J. Wigglesworth III, he should be rolling in dough, too. Unfortunately, his dad was a reporter for the local newspaper and his mom worked part-time at the library, so he hadn't exactly been born with a silver spoon in his mouth.

The only answer was to somehow get the money himself. He grinned, remembering some of the ways he'd tried to get rich quick. He'd had some pretty zany adventures, involving sticky-fingered monkeys, shady characters in velour jumpsuits, and salsa-dancing con artists. Too bad none of his plans had worked.

"It *is* true," said Sid, slapping her hand down on Max's arm before he could take another gumdrop. She leaned across the counter and looked him straight in the eyes. "Max, I'm your best friend in the whole world and I know you don't want to hear this, but someday you're going to have to face the fact that the only way to get money is to get a regular job. Like me. I'm working here at the store this summer so I can save up enough for a brand-new baseball mitt."

Max stared at her blankly. "Get a job?"

Sid closed her eyes and thumped her forehead softly against the countertop. The Brooksville Batters cap that she always wore fell onto the floor. "Yes, Max," came her muffled reply. "A job."

Max blinked. "You mean like a neurosurgeon or an astronaut?"

"No," cried Sid. She lifted her head and glared at him through the curly orange hair that fell across her face. "You're eleven, for goodness' sake. I mean a plain old ordinary job. To pay for things like bowling shoes and movie tickets and ... and ... gumdrops!"

"A job," said Max again, unconvinced.

"Sure," said Sid. "Like babysitting, or being a paperboy!"

Max shuddered. He'd tried the whole paper route thing once. It had nearly killed him.

"No thanks," he said with a grimace. "Do you

know what a paperboy makes in a month? Practically nothing. All that hard work ... and most of the money goes straight to the owner of the newspaper company."

"Okay, then, maybe a different job," said Sid. "Something a little less physically intense. Maybe ..."

"All that money goes straight to the owner," repeated Max. His brain began to buzz the way it did when he was on the verge of a brilliant money-making idea. Slowly, his lips curved into a grin.

Sid gulped. She knew that look. It had gotten her into hot water more times than she could count on both hands. "Now hold on, Max ..."

"The average working Joe has no chance of raking in the big bucks, right?" asked Max. His eyes sparkled with excitement. "All the money goes straight to the top dog. The head honcho. The big cheese."

"The big cheese?" whispered Sid.

"Of course," cried Max. "Why didn't I think of it sooner?" He pushed aside the jar of gumdrops, scooped his three dollars and change back into his pocket and grinned at Sid. "The only way I'm going to get rich is by going into business for myself!"

2 Money Isn't Everything

"Hello, Max," said Sid's mom, gliding through the beaded curtains that separated the front of the store from the storage room. As usual, she wore a floor-length dress made of soft wispy material that floated behind her. She carried several cardboard boxes in her arms, which she plunked down on the counter between Max and Sid.

"Hi, Mrs. Stubberfield," said Max.

"Please, honey, I've told you a million times to call me Bliss," she said with a smile. The sweet scent of ylang-ylang incense followed her into the room.

Max nodded. "Okay," he said, although he knew he probably wouldn't. For as long as he could remember, Sid had called her parents by their first names, Bliss and Ziggy. Max could never call his mom and dad Claire and Maxwell ... it would feel too weird.

"Help yourself to a gumdrop," Bliss offered, nodding to the jar. Exotic bracelets clinked on her wrists as she opened the first box.

Max stuck his tongue out at Sid and reached for another candy.

"So how's the universe treating you, Max?"

asked Bliss as she filled a display case with carob-coated raisins and jalapeno-flavored soy nuts. Her crystal prism earrings threw rainbow reflections on the store walls.

"Pretty good," said Max, eyeing a bag of roasted seaweed. The wrinkly green snack reminded him of the stuff Dad scooped out of the gutters last fall.

"Max has decided to go into business for himself," offered Sid.

"Groovy," said Bliss, pushing the seaweed aside to make room for sun-dried apple chips. "What kind of business?"

"I haven't quite figured that part out yet," admitted Max.

"Max thinks he can get rich faster if he works for himself," Sid added with a smirk.

Bliss laughed. "Money isn't everything."

"Um ... have you met Max?" asked Sid. She ducked as Max fired a red gumdrop at her.

"Let life enrich you," declared Bliss. She flung her arms wide as if she were embracing the entire world. Sid ducked again to avoid being pelted with the fringe on Bliss's sleeve. "Love what you do and do what you love."

"Love doesn't pay the bills," muttered Sid.

"Ziggy and I help people eat food that's good for them and good for our dear Mother Earth," continued Bliss with a serene smile. "So we don't mind if sometimes we barely make enough money to cover our overhead."

"Overhead?" asked Max.

Suddenly, Bliss was all business. Her sparkly purple fingernails tap-tapped on the counter as she rattled off a list. "Overhead – expenses like rent, insurance, and utilities. Property taxes, accounting fees, furniture, and equipment. When you're the boss you have to pay all the bills, organize your product, deal with customers. If you're lucky, you make enough money to pay the mortgage."

Max's shoulders slumped. The buzzing in his brain, which had been raging like a swarm of bumblebees, dwindled to the lazy putt-putt of a housefly. "That sounds awfully complicated."

"Well, you know my motto," Bliss said cheerfully. "You simply can't miss if you follow your ..."

"Bliss," finished Sid. She rolled her eyes at Max, but he was too dejected to smile at the rusty Stubberfield family joke.

Bliss giggled. "Words to live by, Dippy, my dear." She gave Sid a warm hug and kissed her on the top of the head. Max backed away to avoid

14

getting caught in a group smooch.

"Don't call me Dippy," grumbled Sid from beneath several layers of gauzy fabric.

This time Max couldn't help but grin. Bliss was the only person who could call Sid that old nickname and get away with it. Sid's real name was Serendipity Sunshine Stubberfield, and she loathed it. Detested it. In fact, she hated it so much that she was determined to legally change it the minute she was old enough. Whenever Max wanted to get under Sid's skin, he just had to call her Dippy.

"Okay, now why don't you two kids go play," said Bliss. "I'll finish up here."

Sid's eyes lit up. "Great!"

In a flash, Sid whipped off the tie-dyed apron she'd been wearing and snatched her baseball cap off the floor, slapping it on her head backward. She raced out from behind the counter and grabbed Max before Bliss could change her mind. They were halfway to the front door when Bliss's voice floated across the room with one last instruction.

"Don't forget to pick up Zeekie, dear."

Sid groaned as they sailed through the front door.

"Who's Zeekie?" Max asked.

"My cousin," Sid said. "He's spending the

summer with us. I'm supposed to keep him entertained."

"What's so bad about that?" asked Max.

Sid raised one eyebrow and gave Max a pitying look. "You think you've got troubles now? Just wait until you meet Zeekie."

3 Supply and Demand

"Your cousin?" said Max. "Cool!"

Like Sid, Max was an only child. Unlike Sid, sometimes he wished he had another person in the family to talk to and play with. His parents were great, but they had their quirks. His mom was a compulsive organizer – even Max's underwear drawer was color-coordinated – and his dad was an endless fountain of useless bits of information he gathered when writing articles. And they both had the annoying habit of losing track of time and sometimes forgetting Max existed. At least that's what it felt like to Max.

"Zeekie is the total opposite of cool," said Sid with a scowl. "He's probably driven Ziggy insane by now."

Max shrugged. "We can pick him up on the way to my house. I promised my mom I'd help her this afternoon."

"Is the cookie jar full?" asked Sid, immediately cheering up.

Max shrugged again. "Probably."

When she wasn't alphabetizing or organizing, his mom loved to bake ... gooey, fudgy brownies and sticky cinnamon buns and chocolate chip cookies that were more chocolate chip than cookie.

But Max's mind was on his wallet, not his stomach. He was almost certain that becoming an enterprising entrepreneur was his ticket to *mucho* moolah. His buzzing brain had never let him down before. Well, not really.

He could be a self-made millionaire. He saw them all the time on the news. Someone creates a super-fast computer and *bam*! Instant millionaire. Someone else invents a low-fat ice cream and *kapow*! Money in the bank.

"I just have to come up with the right business," he told Sid as they walked down Main Street, passing Daisy's Do's, the hairstylist shop.

Sid looked at him sideways. "Huh?"

"Supply and demand," he said, echoing a phrase he'd heard somewhere. "I need to supply something that people want to pay for. Simple economics."

Sid stopped to look in the window of the Sportz Zone. With a sigh, she stared through the glass at a deluxe catcher's mitt.

"Isn't it a beauty?" she said.

Max glanced at the baseball glove. "Uh huh. What about security? I could be a bodyguard for famous people or deliver diamonds and gold to

18

jewelry stores."

"You'd need a driver's license," said Sid, pressing her nose to the glass. "See the stitching? That's top quality work, you know."

"Archeology?" said Max. "I could dig up fossils, follow old treasure maps, discover ancient civilizations."

"You might want to finish grade school first," Sid said without taking her eyes off the mitt. "You know, I've almost saved up enough money. A few more weeks, and that baby is all mine."

Max was still mulling over business possibilities when he noticed something odd. A bright yellow notice was stapled to the telephone pole in front of the Sportz Zone. There was another one in front of the Bike Shop and Daisy's Do's too. In fact, yellow notices were plastered up and down both sides of Main Street.

"What's with the signs?" he asked Sid, pointing.

"Oh, those?" Sid shrugged. "We have one outside our store too. The mayor wants to give Main Street a face-lift. You know, make it look pretty so more tourists will come. New paint, flowers, whatever."

"Hmmm ..." said Max. The buzzing in his brain kicked up a notch, from drowsy housefly to hungry mosquito.

"There was a big meeting," continued Sid. "All the business owners think it's a good idea, but nobody has the time to do anything about it."

"Really ..." mumbled Max. The hungry mosquito metamorphosed into a demanding dragonfly. This could be just the opportunity he'd been looking for! There had to be a way to make this work for him. But how, exactly?

They left Main Street and went to Sid's house. Max hid a grin as he followed Sid up the path to the front door. White clouds of dandelion fluff scattered into the air with every step. The other houses on the street had neatly trimmed lawns and tidy, orderly flowerbeds. But Ziggy and Bliss didn't believe in pesticides. Or weeding. Or even mowing the grass.

"Cool wind chimes," Max said, gesturing at a cluster of bent knives and forks dangling from a tree limb.

Sid scowled and headed for the front door. Ziggy was famous for his recycled art ... he loved making sculptures out of stuff other people threw away. Unfortunately not everyone appreciated his artistic vision.

"So where's Zeekie?" asked Max. Suddenly, there was a high-pitched whistling sound and something hurtled through the air and struck his left ear. Hard.

"Ahhh!" yelped Max as pain zinged through his skull. He clutched his ear and stumbled backward, tripping over a birdbath fashioned from tomato soup cans and old hubcaps. The back of Max's head hit the ground with a thud.

Slowly, he opened his eyes. The first thing he saw, inches from his nose, was a yellow and black striped boomerang. The second thing he saw was a skinny pair of legs in purple flip-flops. Attached to the skinny legs was a skinny little kid with big ears and glasses, grinning a gap-toothed grin.

"Max," said Sid, "meet Zeekie."

4 Zeekie!

"Oopsy-daisy," said Zeekie. "I guess I need more practice. Most people think boomerangs come from Australia, but did you know that King Tut had a collection of boomerangs? And that the oldest boomerang ever found was 20,000 years old? It was made of mammoth tusk. Isn't that cool?"

Gingerly, Max touched his ear. It felt as if it had been flattened by a semitruck. He groaned.

"Do you know what day it is?" asked Zeekie. He squatted on his heels and peered at Max. "Sometimes people get amnesia when they get hit on the head. Do you know your name? How many fingers am I holding up?"

Max blinked and tried to answer. "Tuesday ... Max ... three ..."

"Are you going to faint?" asked Zeekie. "Can I hang out with you guys today?"

"Um, yes ... I mean no," said Max, confused.

Zeekie opened his mouth. "Will we – "

Sid stepped forward and clamped her hand firmly over his lips. "We're going over to Max's house. You have to leave your boomerang behind."

"I can't," Zeekie said. "It's very special. Did I

tell you it's made out of super high-tech fibers that make it faster than an ordinary boomerang? It's probably the same stuff they make bulletproof vests out of. I'm thinking about being a policeman when I grow up. What do you – "

"Let's just go," broke in Max. He'd just met this kid, but he could tell that if they waited for him to run out of things to say, they'd be here forever. And he had important stuff to do today – like come up with the perfect business plan.

Max and Sid soon discovered that the only way to keep Zeekie from talking their ears off was to keep him out of breath. So they speed-walked the entire way to Max's house. Arms pumping, faces red, they rounded the last corner and marched through the gate, with Zeekie trailing behind.

"Mom," gasped Max, clinging to the porch railing for support. "We're ..."

"Home," wheezed Sid.

"Hello, kids," said Claire Wigglesworth. She knelt in a bed of bright orange and yellow flowers, up to her elbows in mulch. The floppy straw hat on her head made a circle of shade around her, like a portable beach umbrella. "Goodness, you look like you've just run a marathon. Who's your new friend?"

Max's lungs ached. "Zeekie," he managed to say.

"My cousin," added Sid, swiping the back of her hand across her sweaty forehead.

"Howdy," said Zeekie brightly. "Are you Max's mom? Do you always wear such dirty clothes? My mom would freak if I got my clothes that dirty. Did you know that if you put a wax crayon in your pocket and your mom puts it in the dryer, it melts? And guess what? It never comes out!"

Mrs. Wigglesworth brushed at a bit of grass stuck to her elbow. "Really? How interesting."

"Do you only grow flowers in your garden?" asked Zeekie. "Or do you grow vegetables too? My neighbor grows flowers, but my dad says that vegetables are better because you can't eat petunias. Except, did you know that some flowers are edible? It's true. Once my mom put nasturtiums in our salad. Dad called it rabbit food. Have you ever had a pet rabbit? I used to – "

"We're here to help," interrupted Max. He had a feeling he'd be doing a lot of interrupting over the next few weeks.

"Great," said Mrs. Wigglesworth, giving Zeekie a weak smile.

"Why don't you kids grab a snack in the

kitchen and meet me in the backyard?"

Sid grinned. "Yum."

Max watched his mom hurry around the corner of the house, a little faster than necessary, he thought. Then he led the way to the kitchen. Sid made a beeline for the cookie jar.

Zeekie looked around the house, his eyes magnified by his thick glasses. "Where's your bedroom? I used to share a bedroom with my older brother, but then he went away to college so now I have my own room. Do you have bunk beds? I do. I fell off the top bunk when I was five and broke my arm. Have you ever worn a cast? They're itchy and – "

Max glanced helplessly at Sid. She shrugged.

"Do you have a basement?" Zeekie continued. "We do, but I don't like it. It's really dark and smells funny. Have you ever been bitten by a spider? One time I got a spider bite on my toe and it got so swollen I couldn't put on my shoe. Do you like my flip-flops? They're really cool because – "

"Here," said Sid, shoving a cookie into Zeekie's mouth. "Try one."

Max grabbed the milk out of the fridge and poured three glasses. The cookie slowed Zeekie down for a few seconds. Then, crumbs flying, he began chattering about hot air balloons and nimbus cloud formations. Questions pelted against Max's eardrums like hail.

"Hey," said Max, getting an idea. "You should meet my dad. He's a reporter and he loves questions. I bet he'd be interested in your boomerang, too."

"A newspaper reporter or a television reporter?" asked Zeekie. "Once I was on television. Well, my feet were. I was in a parade dressed up like a giant strawberry. What did you dress up for last Halloween? I like Halloween because I like candy, but my mom won't let me eat it all because she says it makes me hyper. Did you know that – "

Max steered Zeekie, still talking, down the hall toward Dad's study. If there was one person who could answer all of Zeekie's questions, it would definitely be Dad. In fact, Max was almost tempted to stay and witness the useless trivia show-down that was sure to occur, but instead he quickly introduced Zeekie to his Dad and tiptoed away, shutting the door behind him.

All Max needed was a few minutes of peace and quiet. If they hurried, he could help mom with her gardening and still have a few minutes left over before Zeekie joined them. Just enough time to come up with a brilliant business plan!

5 Marigold Mania

"Let's get planting," Max told his mom a few moments later in the backyard. The sooner he got this chore over with, the sooner he could do some serious business brainstorming.

Mrs. Wigglesworth set a flat of seedlings on the newspaper-covered picnic table and raised one eyebrow. "What's your hurry?"

Max groaned. "No more questions, please! We don't have much time before Zeekie finds us."

"He does have an inquisitive mind," said Mrs. Wigglesworth. "And a lot of energy."

"Bliss says he runs on solar power," said Sid.

"Enough chitchat!" Max glanced at the house, but there was no sign of Zeekie. Looking back at the picnic table, he saw that the flat was filled with row after row of spiky-leafed plants. There were several more flats on the lawn beside a wheelbarrow full of soil.

"There must be hundreds of them," he said, dismayed.

"About five hundred, to be accurate," Mrs. Wigglesworth replied, brushing her gloves together. "Marigolds. From the genus *Tagetes* of the family *Asteraceae*. I saved my own seeds from last year, but I didn't realize they'd all germinate."

"Where are you going to put them?" asked Sid.

"I just don't know," Mrs. Wigglesworth shrugged helplessly. "I really don't have room for them all. Maybe I can take the extras to my next Green Thumb meeting and give them away."

"Green Thumb?" repeated Sid.

"Our garden club," explained Mrs. Wigglesworth. As president, she arranged the monthly meetings. She also arranged the catering, the newsletters, and the yearly plant show. "I love the garden club, but it's almost too much work for just one person. I'm looking forward to the next meeting so we can elect the new president. Then I can concentrate on my own garden again."

"Hurry, hurry!" urged Max with another glance toward the house. Maybe if they moved fast, they could get the job done and still have time to work on his plan. He grabbed a trowel and shoveled soil into a large terra-cotta pot. Then he reached for a plant.

"Be careful, the roots are quite tender," advised Mrs. Wigglesworth. "Press the soil gently around the stems. Don't crowd them."

"Yeah, yeah," said Max, shaking the young plants out of their temporary plastic pots and plopping them into the large flowerpot. "It's not brain surgery. Tender roots, don't crowd, got it."

Sid rubbed her nose and reached for her own flowerpot. Some of the marigolds were already flowering yellow and orange pom-pom blooms. She rubbed her nose again, then sneezed.

"Bless you," said Mrs. Wigglesworth. "Have you got a cold, dear?"

Sid shrugged. "Allergies. Bliss has me on an allergy-fighting diet. I eat a lot of horseradish."

"Less talking and more transplanting," ordered Max. His flowerpot was full and he pushed it aside. As he reached for a new pot, he noticed the newspaper that was spread over his workspace. He brushed away some soil and looked closer.

"Hey," he said. "This is one of Dad's articles."

"What's it about?" asked Sid, wiping her nose on her sleeve.

Max skimmed the article. His eyes widened and he let out a low whistle. "Holy cow. It says here that Mrs. Camilla Clementine has an orchid that's worth a thousand bucks!"

Mrs. Wigglesworth nodded. "Camilla is a fellow Green Thumb. She has many rare and wonderful specimens in her collection. In fact, she's running for president."

"But a thousand dollars?" persisted Max. "For one single plant?"

"Oh my, yes," she told him. "Vanilla, the world's second most expensive spice, comes from orchids. Your dad wrote an article in the last Green Thumb newsletter about a *Neofinettia falcata*

'Brown Bear' orchid from Japan that sold for $75,000."

Max felt his jaw drop. "Really?"

"It's not just orchids, either," she said, warming to her subject. "Ever hear of Tulipmania? In the early seventeenth century in Holland people went crazy for tulips. They traded their furniture, their jewelry, and even their houses for a single bulb."

Max's brain started buzzing again.

"I can't imagine a world without plants," continued Mrs. Wigglesworth. "We use plants for food and medicine and clothing and glue and inks and cosmetics and oils and paint and paper and soap and wax and really, the list is endless!"

"Cool," said Max.

Mrs. Wigglesworth nodded. "Cool indeed. Horticulture is big business."

A muted crash sounded from the direction of the house, but Max couldn't take his eyes off of the newspaper article. "Big business, huh?" He looked at the hundreds of homeless marigolds still waiting to be planted. He thought of the notices plastered all over Main Street.

Suddenly, the puzzle pieces fit together. Store owners who wanted to beautify Main Street but didn't have time to do it equaled demand. Free marigolds equaled supply. And an endless source of compost and his trusty red wagon equaled zero overhead.

With Sid's help, of course, he could corner the sidewalk flower box industry. Every penny they earned would be pure profit! Why, with all the money they would make they could buy more wagons, hire kids in other towns to work for them, soon they'd be a nation-wide franchise ...

The sound of shattering glass broke into Max's thoughts and a black and yellow boomerang landed at his feet. Zeekie's head popped into view behind the ragged edges of the broken kitchen window.

"Oopsy-daisy," Zeekie said.

6 Open for Business

Mr. Wigglesworth's head popped into view beside Zeekie's. "Sorry," he called out. "My fault."

"Maxwell," gasped Mrs. Wigglesworth. "What on earth were you thinking?"

Mr. Wigglesworth scratched his head. "Well, it's all about aerodynamics, you see ... and I just wanted to try ..."

"Oh, Maxwell," she said as she hurried toward the house. "You're worse than a kid."

"Thank goodness it wasn't Zeekie," whispered Sid to Max. "Fixing that window would have completely wiped out my baseball mitt fund."

"You don't have to worry about saving for that mitt any longer," Max told her with a grin. "We're going to be rolling in green pretty soon."

Sid scratched a mosquito bite on her arm. "Oh really?"

"Yup," said Max. "I've just come up with the most amazingly perfect business plan."

Sid yawned. "Uh huh."

"I'm serious," said Max. The back door opened and Zeekie appeared, his flip-flops flapping down the back steps. Max spoke quickly. "Loads of demand. Zero overhead. All I need is a partner. Are you in?"

Sid squinted at Max. Zeekie trotted closer and closer. Finally Sid shrugged. "Sure, why not? On one condition."

Max gulped. "What condition?"

Zeekie waved the boomerang in the air. "See? I told you it was made of super special high-tech fibers ... it sliced right through that window, no problem-o! Do you think your dad is in trouble, Max? Is he going to fix the window himself? Have you ever used a power drill? My dad has a whole bunch of tools, and – "

Sid raised her voice and jerked her thumb at Zeekie. "If you want me, you get him too. We're a package deal."

"A package deal?" Zeekie turned from Sid to Max. "Are we going on a trip? Once my mom got a deal on a cruise to Alaska, but she didn't take me along. It's cold in Alaska. Especially in the winter. Did you know that sometimes ninety percent of an iceberg floats underwater? Are we – "

Max tuned Zeekie out. His idea was a sure thing, but he couldn't do it alone. He needed Sid's help. Even if that meant her motormouth cousin was part of the bargain.

"Fine," he said, interrupting Zeekie yet again. "He's in. Do we have a deal? Are we business partners?"

Sid grinned. "You bet! I was wondering how I'd keep Zeekie entertained for a whole summer." She stuck out her arm and they shook hands. "Partners."

Zeekie squinted at them through his glasses. "Partners?" he asked. "What kind of partners? What business? What are you guys talking about?"

Sid laughed. "For once, I think Zeekie is asking all the right questions. Exactly what have I gotten myself into this time?"

"Is it a surprise?" Zeekie grinned and jiggled from one foot to the other. "Do you want me to guess? Are we going to have a lemonade stand? Sell cookies? Mow lawns? Walk dogs? What's the plan, Max? Huh? Huh? What's the plan?"

Max clutched his head. "Quiet!"

Zeekie's mouth snapped shut.

Max was quickly changing his mind about wanting a little cousin of his own. "If you can stop asking questions for just five minutes," he said through clenched teeth, "I'll tell you all about it. Time is money, you know."

Sid grabbed Zeekie by the elbow and they sat

at the picnic table. Max collected his thoughts. This was his very first staff meeting, and he wanted to do it right. He wished he had a briefcase. That would be much more businesslike. And an overhead projector and one of those pointy laser lights so that he could give a proper business proposal presentation. All he had was a garden trowel, however, so he picked it up, cleared his throat, and pointed at the marigolds.

"What do you see?" he asked.

"Plants?" piped up Zeekie. "Flowers? Leaves? Dirt? Air? Molecules?"

"No, no, no," said Max. "Profit."

"I don't get it," said Sid. Even Zeekie looked stumped.

"We," said Max, thumping the trowel handle on the picnic table for emphasis, "are going into the traveling flowerbox business."

Sid crossed her arms over her chest and fired a question of her own at Max. "Demand?"

"Main Street needs a face-lift," Max fired back.

"Company name?" asked Sid.

"Er ... Grow 'n' Go," said Max, thinking fast.

"Overhead?" she continued. "Equipment?"

"The marigolds are free," said Max. "Mom's special guaranteed-to-make-anything-

grow compost is free. Water is free. They provide the pots, we provide the plants. No overhead. Zip, zero, *nada*."

"Customer base?" questioned Sid.

"Every business on Main Street," answered Max. "Daisy's Do's, the Bike Shop, the Sportz Zone, your parents' store, maybe even the police station. We'll ask them all."

"Transportation?"

"My red wagon," Max replied without missing a beat. "We'll fill it with plants and dirt. Once the flowerboxes are planted, we'll make the rounds once or twice a week to water and weed."

"I can't believe I'm saying this," Sid said, uncrossing her arms at last. "But for once you've come up with an idea that sounds like it might actually work!"

Max grinned. His business proposal was a success! Now that Sid was on board, all he had to do was put his plan into action. There were a million details to iron out ... he needed to evaluate and organize and strategize, maybe even draw up a flowchart or two.

It was time to get down to business!

7 Sign on the Dotted Line

Max set his alarm to go off extra early the next morning. He ate breakfast, showered, and was dressed in his Sunday suit and tie before his parents were even out of bed. He found a wrinkled package of instant hot chocolate in the back of the pantry, then headed out to the backyard to wait for Sid and Zeekie.

"The early bird catches the worm," he told himself, setting his steaming mug on the picnic table beside Dad's battered briefcase. He had borrowed it temporarily, just until he could buy himself a snazzy new one.

Today was the grand opening of Grow 'n' Go. Max ran through his to-do list. There were customers to talk to, equipment to gather, plants to take care of. It was a good thing he had dependable employees. He pushed up his suit cuff and glanced at his watch. While he waited, he picked up the metal watering can. Product quality was top priority. Nobody liked droopy flowers.

An eerie, familiar whistling noise filled the air. It grew louder and louder, and before Max could figure out which direction it was coming from, the watering can exploded out of his hand. It pinwheeled into the air, spraying water. Only when it crashed to earth did Max spot the boomerang in the grass nearby.

"Oopsy-daisy," sang Zeekie, trotting around the corner. Sid followed a few steps behind, her lips set in a grim line.

"Sorry we're late," Sid said. "Time being money and all that." She glanced at Max's outfit. "Nice suit, dude."

"I'm dressed for success," replied Max with a frown. He touched his hair to see if the goopy gel he'd borrowed from Mom's bathroom was doing its job. It smelled kind of funny, but he thought the slicked-back hairdo made him look more grown-up.

Zeekie scooped up his boomerang and shoved it into the back pocket of his baggy shorts. "Morning, Boss! Are we going to start our new business today? What do you want me to do? I'm really strong, you know. I bet I could lift you up. Want me to try? Once, at school, I lifted up a grade two-er and – "

"Today," announced Max, "we're going to concentrate on phase one of my business plan. Marketing."

"Marketing?" repeated Sid.

Max popped open the briefcase and reached inside for a stack of business cards. He'd stayed up late last night making them on Dad's computer. He admired one, then handed it to Sid.

"Marketing," he explained, "means letting people know about our business. Creating a buzz."

"Like television commercials?" asked Zeekie. "I was on TV once – "

"Yeah, I remember, big parade, giant strawberry, yada yada yada," Max interrupted him. "Commercials cost too much, but you've got the right idea. I thought we'd spread the word by targeting our potential consumers and approaching them directly with verbal communication."

"You mean go talk to them," Sid said.

Max frowned. "Well, yeah. I guess you could put it that way. Anyway, I made enough business cards to hand out to all the stores on Main Street. Plus I made up these cool informational product description brochures."

"Good grief," snorted Sid. "Where are you coming up with all this executive mumbo jumbo?"

"I guess being an entrepreneur just comes naturally to me," Max said modestly. He touched his gleaming, if somewhat greasy, locks. "I have a good head for business."

Sid rolled her eyes and reached into the briefcase for a flyer. She spied the corner of a book under the papers and yanked it out. "*Profit, Profit, Profit: How to Start Your Own Business and Become a Millionaire in 157 Easy Steps,*" she read out loud.

"Uh, that's just research," Max said, grabbing the book. He stuffed it deeper into the briefcase. "Here's a brochure."

Sid looked at the folded paper. Then she looked closer at the business card. "They're nice, Max, but I thought this was a partnership. How come only your name is on here?"

Max waved the question away. "You're on there too."

"Maxamillian J. Wigglesworth III," Sid read aloud. She squinted at the fine print. "And associates."

"See?" said Max. Sid opened her mouth to protest, but Max quickly added, "So who's ready to sell, sell, sell?"

"I am," piped up Zeekie. "My grandpa says I'm a natural born salesman. He says I could talk the ear off a cob of corn. Except, I don't really like corn. It gets caught between my teeth. How many teeth have you lost? Did you ever forget to put a tooth under your pillow for the tooth fairy? Once, I – "

"Okay," said Max, snapping the briefcase shut. "I think this concludes our meeting. It's time to take this show on the road!"

Their first stop was the Vegetarian Deli. Max sneaked one last glance at his slicked-back hairdo in the store window before striding confidently through the front door. Haunting Australian didgeridoo music played softly in the background.

"Hi, kids, help yourselves," Bliss greeted them, pointing to the gumdrop jar.

"No thanks, ma'am," Max answered politely. "We're here today because we have an exciting business proposal for you."

"*Ma'am?* This sounds serious." Bliss sat on the stool behind the counter and gave Max her complete attention. "Okay, tell me all about it."

Taking a deep breath, Max launched into the sales pitch he'd practiced so carefully in front of the bathroom mirror last night. He followed all the rules in chapter four of "*Profit, Profit, Profit!*" He made eye contact with the client. He used buzzwords like *professional* and *proficient* and *pesticide-free*. And most importantly, he oozed confidence and enthusiasm. The shiny hair helped.

At first Bliss looked skeptical, but then, slowly, she began to smile. By the time Max handed her a brochure with the prices on it, she seemed impressed.

"So you do all the work?" she said.

Max nodded. "Yes, ma'am. One hundred percent."

"All the weeding?" she asked. "And the watering?"

"Everything," Max said. "All you do is supply the container. We'll take care of the rest."

"I think you've just landed your very first customer," she said, reaching for a pen. "Where do I sign?"

8 Phase Two

Soon they had a total of eight newly signed contracts. Max was thrilled. Everybody loved the idea. Go 'n' Grow's stock ... if he actually had any ... was going right through the roof!

Back at Max's house, Zeekie went inside to chat with Mr. Wigglesworth, but Max and Sid continued around back to their "office." Max opened his briefcase on the picnic table and studied their new client list.

"That was a productive morning," he said, loosening his tie with one hand. "The only person who didn't sign up was Mrs. Clementine."

"She *does* own the flower shop," said Sid, sprawled in the hammock a few feet away. "What would people think if 'Blooms and Blossoms' couldn't take care of their own flower box?"

"Yeah, but would it kill her to smile once in a while?" Max asked. "If I had a thousand-dollar plant sitting at home, you wouldn't be able to pry the grin off my face."

"Maybe she'd have been nicer if Zeekie hadn't knocked over those glass vases," Sid reminded him.

"Stupid boomerang," muttered Max. "Besides,

we promised to pay her back with next week's profit. Anyway, eight clients is a fine customer base to build our business on. We'll get started right after lunch."

Sid sat upright in the hammock. "Today? But we worked all morning. It's summer ... when do we get to have fun?"

"Time is money." Max snapped his briefcase shut. "The dictionary is the only place where money comes before work."

"What about lunch?" whined Sid. "Even workaholics take coffee breaks."

"I'm going to change my clothes," he said, heading for the house. "Rest while I'm gone!"

Sid was still frowning when Max returned a few minutes later with Zeekie in tow.

"It's time for phase two," Max announced. Gone was his suit and tie. Now he wore his mom's gardening apron over his T-shirt and shorts. It was a little oversized, but it had handy-dandy pockets for gloves and clippers and spades and twine and anything else Max might need today.

"What's phase two?" asked Zeekie.

Max grinned, a long-handled shovel in each hand. "Inventory."

"The flowers are right here." Sid crossed her

arms over her chest and glared at him. "What other inventory could we possibly have?"

"A motivated worker is a productive worker," Max muttered under his breath. He'd read that in chapter fourteen of *Profit, Profit, Profit!* "I propose a deal," he said out loud. "Inventory first, then we'll stop for lunch. Mom made chocolate cupcakes."

"With frosting?" asked Sid.

Max held out a shovel. "Yup."

Sid sighed and took it. "Point me in the direction of this mysterious inventory."

Max grabbed the handle of his wagon and led them behind Mom's potting shed. "Behold," he said dramatically. "Our inventory."

Sid and Zeekie stared at the inventory. Or, to be more precise, they stared at Mrs. Wigglesworth's compost pile.

It wasn't any ordinary compost pile. This particular compost pile was Mrs. Wigglesworth's pride and joy. Every kitchen scrap, every fallen leaf, every blade of clipped grass found its way here, where it stewed, rotting and decomposing until it turned into rich, black earth. Normally Max stayed as far away from it as humanly possible, but today he was seeing it in a whole new light.

"Black gold," he whispered to himself.

Zeekie had only one question. "What stinks?"

Max waved away an annoying fly. "That, my friend, is the smell of money. I'll hold the wagon steady. You two dig in!"

Sid slapped at two flies buzzing around her legs. "Are you sure your mom doesn't mind?"

Max swatted at a couple more flies. "Nope. I think this is the first idea of mine that she's really liked. In fact, she invited us all to her boring old Green Thumb election tomorrow night, but I said we'd be too busy."

Sid poked the pile with the tip of her shovel. A cloud of black flies scattered, only to return seconds later. Something with a lot of legs skittered farther under a slimy lettuce leaf. "What's this? Baloney? And fried chicken?"

"I added a few extra ingredients last night," Max admitted. "Just to give it a little power boost."

"You're not supposed to put meat in the compost!" Sid poked the pile again. "No wonder it smells so bad."

"Dig deeper," urged Max, brushing a fly off his nose. "The good stuff is at the bottom."

"I bet it's loaded with arthropods," grinned Zeekie. "Millipedes and sowbugs and black beetles. Did you know that insects are older than dinosaurs? And there's about a quintillian insects in the world today? That's a billion billion. Did you know that some people eat insects? I ate a caterpillar once, but it was an accident. Have you – "

"Please stop," groaned Sid. She used her shovel to push aside a rotten tomato. A thick brown earthworm squirmed deeper into the pile. "I might lose my lunch, and we haven't even eaten yet!"

9 All Kinds of Muscles

Once the last shovelful of compost was in the wagon they hurried back to the picnic table, hoping to leave the smell – and the flies – behind.

Max pulled a small spiral notebook out of his gardening apron and flipped it open. "Great job. That's one more thing to check off our list."

"*Our* list? *Zeekie* and *I* did all the work," complained Sid.

"Yeah," piped up Zeekie. "Digging is hard. My arms hurt. And my shoulders. Did you know there are over seven hundred muscles in the human body?"

"The brain is a muscle, too," retorted Max. He tapped the list with his pen. "It's hard work coming up with all these ideas."

Sid craned her neck. "Exactly how long *is* that list?"

Max smiled and stuck the notebook back in the pocket. "Let management worry about the details," he told her. A single black fly buzzed around his head.

"Listen, Max," began Sid. "Don't you think you're getting a little carried away – "

A low humming filled the air.

"What's that sound?" asked Max. He waved away several more flies attempting to land in his hair. Sid and Max both glared at Zeekie.

"It's not me." Zeekie pointed at his boomerang, safely in his back pocket. The humming noise grew louder.

"That's weird," said Max. He used both hands to swat at the insects that circled his head like the rings on a planet. "Where did all these flies come from?"

Sid and Zeekie glanced at each other and took several steps back. The flies ignored them. "They must have followed us from the compost pile," Sid said.

Max hopped up and down and flapped his arms about his ears. Still more flies came.

"It's your hair!" Sid shouted through the frantic buzzing.

"Help!" cried Max.

Zeekie whipped out his boomerang. "I bet I can hit them!"

"No!" Sid dropped her shovel and grabbed Zeekie's arm. "Follow me."

Through the cloud of flies, Max saw them race away. "Wait," he cried, trailing after them.

"You can't leave me. I'm the boss! I order you to help me!"

Arms flapping, he rounded the corner of the house, only to be stopped dead in his tracks by a blast of cold water.

"*Urg ... ack*," he sputtered, falling to his knees.

"It's working," he heard Sid say through the water roaring in his ears.

She was right. Soon the last fly was gone. Zeekie ran to turn off the tap, and Sid dropped the garden hose on the ground.

"Are you okay?" she asked.

Max wiped a wet clump of hair out of his eyes. Every trace of his high-powered hairdo was hosed away. "Maybe now *would* be a good time to stop for lunch."

Sid giggled. "Good. All that exercise brought back my appetite."

Soon they were sitting at the kitchen table, munching on sandwiches and slurping lemonade. Sid took a big bite of her third frosted cupcake and sighed happily.

"Why couldn't we go into a good business?" she asked, licking a glob of icing off her thumb. "Like making cupcakes? Something I could really sink my teeth into!"

"Grow 'n' Go *is* a good idea," Max insisted. "The flies were just a freaky accident."

"So what's next, boss?" asked Zeekie. "Can I be in charge of the watering can? Huh? Can I? Because plants can't live without water, right? Although, did you know that there are hundreds of plants that need practically no water at all? It's true! Some dessert plants have hairy leaves, to help stop evaporation. And – "

Max pulled out his spiral notebook and thumbed through it. "The next thing on my list is to fill the flower boxes with compost."

"I'm starting to hate that list," grumbled Sid.

"Organization is the key to success," said Max, "And Grow 'n' Go is going to be my most successful idea ever."

After lunch they hauled the compost to Main Street. Max whistled a jaunty tune as Sid and Zeekie took turns pulling the heavy wagon.

"Let's start here," Max said, stopping in front of Bliss and Ziggy's store. "We can work our way up the street."

"Sounds like a plan," agreed Sid, wiping beads of sweat off her forehead. She turned her baseball cap around so the brim shaded her nose, which was beginning to turn pink.

"Boy, is it hot!" Zeekie wiggled out of his shirt and twisted it around his head like a turban. "Have you ever fried an egg on the sidewalk? I tried last summer, but it didn't work. Too many dogs. Do you like to cook? One time I – "

"Yeah, yeah," interrupted Max. "Enough talk. After all, time is – "

"Money," chorused Sid and Zeekie together.

Max grinned. "That's right. Grab a shovel. We've got eight flower boxes to fill."

"Where?" asked Zeekie.

Max looked around. "Good question."

There were plenty of Ziggy's far-out sculptures in front of the store, but nothing looked remotely like a flowerpot. Nothing, except ...

"Oh no," groaned Sid. She pointed at a large cast-iron claw-foot bathtub. "Ziggy found that at the dump. You know how my parents are about recycling. Reduce, reuse, recycle ... no matter how ugly it is."

Max gulped. The tub was enormous! "You don't think − "

The front door jingled as Bliss stepped outside. "Isn't it wonderful?" she said, clasping her hands together delightedly. The silver rings on her thumbs winked in the bright sunlight.

"It's big," Max said.

"Can you believe someone threw away this lovely antique? I can't wait to see it filled with flowers!" gushed Bliss. "And the best part is, when everybody saw it, they wanted unique ways to plant their flowers, too!"

Max glanced up the street. The Bike Shop had a huge rubber tire outside its front door, waiting to be filled. The Sportz Zone had a giant plastic picnic cooler and the hardware store had not one but two jumbo-sized red toolboxes. Max's heart sank down to his toes.

"This is going to take forever," he groaned.

10 Working Hard for the Money

It took five more wagonloads of compost, six more of regular garden soil from Max's mom's garden, and another two trips to bring all the marigolds to Main Street. Even Max had to take a turn pulling the wagon. By the time they were ready to plant, they felt about as energetic as overcooked noodles.

"*Urgg*," groaned Max, leaning against the tub, too tired to blink.

"*Glrgg*," moaned Sid. Her shirt was streaked with sweat and dirt.

"Need ... water ..." gasped Zeekie. He lay prone on the sidewalk, forcing passers-by to step over his body.

Max nudged the canteen toward Zeekie with his toe. After the third trip they'd gotten smart and grabbed some water and slapped on some sunscreen. Back and forth they'd trudged, like camels crossing the dessert over and over and over again. Zeekie had surprised Max by working steadily without complaint.

"Can we go home?" mumbled Sid.

Max didn't have the energy to reach for his

spiral notebook. "We still have to plant the marigolds. It's on the list."

Zeekie drank deeply. He wiped his mouth on the back of his hand and sighed. "Can't we do it tomorrow?"

Max wanted to say yes. He wanted to crawl into the hammock with an ice-cold lemonade and a comic book. Something was definitely wrong here. He was supposed to be the brains of this operation, not the brawn. Head honchos didn't sweat. Big cheeses didn't haul dirt until their arms wanted to fall off. He wiped the perspiration out of his eyes and felt like giving up.

Then he thought of the contracts in his brief-case. "Sorry, Zeekie, but we promised these people. And the first rule of good business is always keep your promises. Even if it is hard work."

So they planted. They filled the bathtub with marigolds. They filled the cooler and the two tool-boxes and all the other containers on Main Street. Only after the last marigold was planted did Max step back and survey the street.

The results were astonishing. Orange and yellow marigolds nodded their heads in the slight breeze, making the street seem brighter and friendlier somehow. In spite of his aching back,

Max stood a little straighter. "Looks good." Sid sneezed, rubbed her nose with a dirty hand, and sneezed again.

"Maybe you should go to the doctor," suggested Zeekie. "They can give you allergy medicine. Did you know some people are allergic to sunshine? It's true! They can't go outside in the sun and they have to ..."

"Bliss is trying something new," said Sid tiredly. "Broccoli, walnuts, and chili peppers. It should kick in any time now."

"*Mmmmm* ... broccoli," joked Max.

Sid glared at him. "Funny. You know what? I

don't care what's on that list of yours, I'm taking a break. There's more to life than making money."

"But we haven't watered," said Zeekie. "Max put me in charge of watering, remember?"

Max sighed. The watering can was at home. In his backyard. Far, far from Main Street. He hesitated, then made an executive decision. "You stay here," he told Sid. "Come on, Zeekie. One more trip for us."

They trudged back to the Wigglesworth house for the fourteenth time. Even Zeekie was too tired to talk. Max loaded the watering can onto the wagon. Silently, he watched Zeekie fill the watering can with the garden hose. And, still without speaking, they turned around and trudged back toward Main Street.

Max stared at his feet. Right, left, right, left. Being the boss of his own company was turning out to be a lot more work than he'd thought. Where was his air-conditioned corner office? Or the private Jacuzzi and the company jet? This was a billion times worse than being a paper boy. He hadn't worked this hard in ... well, ever!

Back at the store, Sid sipped on a mango smoothie and watched Max grab the heavy watering can. To everyone's surprise, it lifted effortlessly.

"It's empty!" Max held the watering can above his head and shook it. A few drops fell onto his face, making clean tracks on his dusty skin.

"I filled it right to the top," said Zeekie. "You saw me."

Max glanced at the wagon. A wet, wavy line trailed along the sidewalk behind them. He turned the watering can upside down and inspected it. There, below the dent made by Zeekie's boomerang, was a tiny crack.

Zeekie gulped. "Oopsy-daisy."

Max didn't know whether to yell or cry. Before he could do either, Mrs. Clementine crossed the street toward them.

"I've been watching you," she said. "Here. There's a water spigot behind my store."

Max saw the watering can in her hand and felt his spirits lift. Maybe he had judged her too quickly. "Gee, thanks!"

Mrs. Clementine handed the can to Zeekie, who quickly hid his boomerang behind his back. "Don't break it."

Max forced himself to say, "Yes, ma'am."

"If you're serious about this business of yours," Mrs. Clementine continued, "you might want to become a Green Thumb member."

61

With that, she turned and strode back to her store.

"Can we go to a meeting?" asked Zeekie. "Please? I have so many questions. Like how fast can a Venus flytrap digest a fly? And if you push a bean seed up your nose, will it really grow?"

"Forget it," Max said. "I'm not wasting a whole evening with a bunch of boring old grouches."

"But Max," said Sid. "What about networking? Wouldn't that be good for the business?"

"We don't have time for that," Max answered. "Besides, we've already done all the hard work. It's clear sailing from now on."

11 Bathtubs and Cat Poop

"Another day, another dollar," yawned Max. He'd had a good night's sleep, and now he was ready to get back in the trenches. He threw back the covers, sat up in bed, and immediately collapsed back onto his pillow.

His back hurt. His legs felt like bricks. His arms ached. Taking a deep breath, he sat up again. Slowly. Muscles he didn't even know he had screamed out in agony. Clutching the headboard for support, he pulled himself to his feet and hobbled to the bathroom.

Ten minutes in a steaming shower helped loosen his tightly clenched muscles, and by the time he was halfway to Sid's house, he was almost walking like a normal boy again, instead of a ninety-year-old man.

Sid and Zeekie were waiting for him on the front step.

"Hi, guys," Max said. He would have raised his hand in a wave, but his shoulders still hurt. Sid and Zeekie didn't wave either, he noticed. "Ready for phase three?"

"What's phase three?" asked Zeekie.

Wincing, Max reached into the gardening apron for his notebook. "Maintenance. Don't worry," he added, seeing Sid frown, "This is the easy part."

"It better be," said Sid. "I'm so sore I could barely lift my toast this morning."

"It hurt to brush my teeth," said Zeekie.

"I'm a little sore, too," admitted Max. He reached out and gingerly helped them to their feet. "Today will be easier, I promise."

Max felt his spirits rise as the three of them walked to Main Street. It was true. The hardest part *was* behind them. All they had to do now was water the plants, maybe pull a weed or two, and collect their weekly fees. He grinned as they reached the Vegetarian Deli.

One look at the bathtub, however, wiped the grin off his face. Someone, or something, had dug a hole right in the middle of it. Crushed marigolds bordered the crater. A few plants lay on the sidewalk, wilting in the morning sun. Several of the other containers had holes, too.

"Sabotage!" cried Max. "A jealous competitor, trying to ruin our business!"

"Or maybe cats," suggested Zeekie.

"Cats?" scoffed Max. "*Pul-leaze*. This is obviously the work of international corporate spies. They're trying to muscle in on my territory, steal my customers – "

"Poop in your flowerbeds," finished Zeekie.

Max blinked. "Huh?"

Zeekie pointed. "Cat poop."

"*Oooh*, gross!" Sid wrinkled her nose. "Brooksville has loads of stray cats. How are we supposed to stop them from digging up our flowers?"

"I'll stand guard," offered Zeekie. He grinned. "I knew my night vision goggles would come in handy. Do you think Aunty Bliss will let me stay up all night?"

"Nobody's staying up all night," Max said. His head was spinning, but not in a good way. "There has to be a simple answer."

"I bet they'd know at the Green Thumb meeting," said Zeekie.

"Yeah," agreed Sid. "Maybe they could tell us what these funny little bugs are, too."

"Bugs?" gulped Max. He followed her outstretched finger and noticed tiny insects crawling on one of the marigolds. While he watched, they spread to the next plant. Max could almost hear their miniscule jaws chewing through his profit margin.

Sid and Zeekie waited expectantly.

Finally Max threw his hands up in defeat. "All right! We'll go to the meeting. But don't blame me if it's one big yawn-fest!"

12 Election Night

"Hurry, children," urged Mrs. Wigglesworth. "Tonight is a very special Green Thumb meeting and I don't want to be late."

They walked past a glass greenhouse, climbed the steps leading to the front door, and watched Mrs. Wigglesworth press the doorbell. A moment later the door swung open.

"So kind of you to come," Mrs. Clementine said, glancing pointedly at her watch. "The meeting will be starting shortly."

"Wipe your feet, children," Mrs. Wigglesworth said. Max thought she sounded nervous. With a start, he realized that even adults were scared of Mrs. Clementine.

Inside, there were plants everywhere ... lined up on the piano, balanced on the fireplace mantle, and hanging from the ceiling. Several Green Thumb members milled about, eating and talking quietly.

"Snacks!" said Sid, making a beeline for the refreshment table.

Max ignored the food. This was such a waste of time. He could be crunching the numbers or thinking outside the box or whatever company executives did at night.

"It's about time old Clemmy hosted one of these meetings," said a gray-haired man with tea biscuit crumbs in his mustache. "You'd think she was the Queen of England, the way she puts on airs."

Max looked up, surprised. Two men stood with their backs to him, stuffing dainty sandwiches into their mouths. Max pretended to be interested in the marble fireplace.

"Maybe she was afraid you'd bust one of her fancy teacups, George," teased his friend. "This place is like a museum."

Max recognized George Digsby, the owner of the Sportz Zone. He was famous for his huge pumpkins. In fact, he held Brooksville's record for growing the biggest pumpkin ever. Max's dad had done a front-page story on it.

"Yeah, everything in it is old and dusty. Just like the owner," grumbled George.

"Grouchy old coot," laughed the man. "You know, with both you and Camilla running for Green Thumb president tonight, you might want to turn on the charm if you're looking for votes."

"*Hrumph*," snorted George. "I just want to see

this orchid she's been bragging about. Who ever heard of a thousand-dollar flower? Ridiculous."

"Jealous?" teased his friend. "Nobody's talking about your prize winning pumpkin anymore."

Before George could answer, a bell rang sharply. Everybody turned to Mrs. Clementine. Her dress was perfectly starched and every hair was in its place. A small table stood beside her, holding something draped in a lace cloth.

"Welcome, fellow Green Thumbs," she said. "Before we begin the voting process, I'd like to take this opportunity to share my greatest achievement ..."

"Quit showing off," heckled George. "Show us the silly flower already."

"Real mature," whispered Sid.

"Maybe he's got a secret crush on her," Zeekie whispered back. "Like that boy at the swimming pool, remember? The one who kept calling you carrot-head and followed you around all day? Aunty Bliss says it's because he really likes you and ..."

Sid clapped her hand over Zeekie's mouth. "Zip it!"

Mrs. Clementine cleared her throat and reached for the edge of the cloth. "As I was saying, it's my pleasure to reveal to you my pride and joy, the result of my life's work with orchids, a plant I call *Victor Invictus* ..."

Suddenly, the lights went out. Teacups crashed to the floor. Thuds and shouts rang out as people bumped into each other in the blackness.

"What's happening?" cried a woman's voice.

"*Ooof,*" grunted a man. "My foot!"

Max felt something grab his arm. He opened his mouth to yell when he heard Sid's voice.

"Max, is that you?"

"Yeah," he said, swallowing hard. "Are you okay?"

"I've got Zeekie," said Sid. "What's going on?"

Before Max could offer a guess, the lights flickered, then flashed back on. Green Thumb members blinked at each other, looking dazed and confused.

A horrible scream ripped through the air. It only took a moment for Max to realize the scream was coming from Mrs. Clementine.

Victor Invictus lay crumpled on the floor, completely ruined.

"My poor Victor!" Mrs. Clementine moaned. "Murdered!"

"Now Camilla," said Mrs. Wigglesworth, offering the distraught woman a glass of water. "I'm sure it was just an accident." The Green Thumb members had left, *Victor Invictus* had been swept up, and the house was now quiet.

"An accident?" cried Mrs. Clementine. "Are you daft?"

"Don't get mad at Mom," protested Max. "It's not her fault."

Mrs. Clementine took another sip of water. "Perhaps not," she said archly. "But somebody is clearly to blame for this tragedy. And I think we all know who that somebody is. A certain jealous competitor, perhaps."

"Just because George is running against you doesn't mean he'd do something like this," said Mrs. Wigglesworth. She patted Mrs. Clementine's arm soothingly. "I know this evening was upsetting. We'll postpone the election until you're feeling better."

"He'd do anything to become Green Thumb

president instead of me," muttered Mrs. Clementine.

"Perhaps we'd better go now, children," said Mrs. Wigglesworth. "I'll phone you in the morning, Camilla. I'm so sorry about your orchid."

"Maybe you can grow another one," suggested Zeekie. "Maybe – "

Mrs. Clementine frowned and Zeekie closed his mouth.

Later, in the car, Zeekie chatted about lightning storms and how to get electricity from a potato. Sid leaned closer to Max.

"And you thought this meeting would be boring," she whispered.

Max reviewed the night in his head. He remembered the conversation by the fireplace. And the suspiciously well-timed blackout. He felt the gears inside his brain rev up. Did George really want to be president badly enough to destroy Mrs. Clementine's orchid? And if so, why risk doing it with so many people in the room? It didn't make any sense.

"Too bad about the orchid," Sid said. She pulled a folded napkin out of her pocket and bit into a lemon tart. "The food was good, though."

Max nodded, distracted.

Sid licked lemon filling off her fingers and scrunched the napkin into a ball. "The worst part is we didn't find out how to stop the cats from pooping in our flowers."

"You're wrong, Sid," he said. "The worst part is that a thousand-dollar plant got murdered tonight, right under our noses!"

"You don't think the lights went out by accident?" asked Sid.

Max shook his head. "Nope. I don't believe in coincidences."

Sid shrugged. "The grown-ups will figure it out."

"Maybe," said Max. "Or maybe they need a little help."

"Whoa," said Sid. "We're in the traveling flower box business, remember? Between poopy cats and leaky watering cans, we don't have time to solve a mystery."

"True," agreed Max. "But I've been thinking ..."

"Uh oh," groaned Sid. "I hate it when you do that."

Max ignored her. "Mrs. Clementine wants to know who murdered Victor, right?"

"Right, but – "

"So what if we solve the case?" Max's brain was going full throttle now. "Maybe there will be a reward. Maybe a really big reward. Maybe she'll feel so grateful that she'll let us have some of Victor's seeds or whatever. Maybe we can grow dozens of junior Victors, and sell them to the highest bidders, and ..."

"That's a lot of 'maybes,'" Sid told him. "We don't know who wrecked her orchid, or how or even why. Where would we start?"

Max grinned. "With our prime suspect ... Mr. George Digsby."

14 The Big Picture

The next morning, Max headed to Main Street extra early to weed and water the marigolds. He wore the gardening apron, as usual, but today he'd added a few extra items to its many pockets. Things that might come in handy on a murder investigation.

"I'm ready to water," said Zeekie when he and Sid arrived.

"Already done," Max told him.

Zeekie looked disappointed. "What else is on the list? Should I weed? Patrol for cat poop? Check for bugs?"

"Done, done, and done," said Max. He reached into the apron and pulled out his dad's two-way walkie-talkies. They were almost as old as Bliss's bathtub, but they worked. "Today we've got a different job to do."

Sid raised an eyebrow at the low-tech gizmos. "What're those for?"

"Surveillance," Max said. "We're going to figure out what happened to that orchid."

"But how?" questioned Zeekie. "And why? And what about Go 'n' Grow? I thought we were gardeners, not detectives."

Max didn't want to admit it, but being the CEO of Go 'n' Grow was quickly losing its appeal. It suddenly seemed like a whole lot of work for not a whole lot of money. You water a plant, and the next day it's dry again. You pull a weed, and another grows in its place. Max shuddered at the thought of spending the rest of the summer watering and weeding.

"Think of it as an exciting business opportunity," he suggested. "Maybe we can expand into the exotic orchid market. That's where the real money is. You need to look at the big picture."

"I don't know," said Zeekie. He flicked a bug off of a marigold leaf. "I think our plants need us."

"They'll be fine," Max assured him. "Now, let's start with our prime suspect."

"Right," said Sid. "George Digsby. Is there any way I can talk you out of this, Max?"

Max shook his head. "Nope!"

"Then I might as well tell you what Bliss told me," she said with a sigh.

Max grinned eagerly. "You have information? A clue, perhaps?"

"Bliss told me that years ago, George and Camilla used to be sweethearts," began Sid. She gave a little sigh. "It's really kind of romantic."

"*Ewww*," said Max.

"I told you!" cried Zeekie. "It's true love! Did you know that bald eagles mate for life? And that they really aren't bald at all? In fact, their head feathers don't turn white until they are four or five years old and – "

"Then one day, they had a huge fight and broke off their engagement. They've been rivals ever since," continued Sid.

"Like when Mrs. Clementine opened her flower shop a few years ago, and George opened his sporting goods store two months later, right across the street," said Max.

"Right," said Sid. "And last Christmas George put a Santa and reindeer on his store roof, and the next day Mrs. Clementine had an entire nativity scene complete with a live goat."

Zeekie scratched his chin. "Do you think George was jealous of the orchid? Jealous enough to murder it?"

"Let's find out," replied Max.

They began their surveillance at George's store. Whistling a casual tune, Max pretended to scoop cat poop out of the picnic cooler flower bed. He glanced up and down the street, then tucked his chin to his chest.

"Coast is clear," he whispered into his walkie-talkie.

"Roger that," came Sid's reply from her position in the back alley.

Across the street, Zeekie lounged against a lamppost. He gave Max a slight nod, which Max returned.

They waited.

And waited.

Finally, Max's apron crackled. He fished out the walkie-talkie.

"Subject is on the move!" came Sid's hoarse whisper. "I'm in pursuit."

Max signaled Zeekie and they dashed behind the stores. Sure enough, George Digsby was already halfway down the alley. Max spotted Sid a few steps behind, slinking from garbage can to garbage can, and he and Zeekie hurried to catch up.

It was nearly impossible to stay out of sight when George turned onto a side street. With only the occasional bush or mailbox to use for cover, Max was sure that George would notice them. But on George marched, looking neither left nor right. People watched them curiously, some even waved, but George kept walking, never once noticing Max, Sid, and Zeekie hot on his heels.

When they turned down a third street, Max felt his stomach tighten with excitement. Mrs. Clementine's hedge loomed ahead. George Digsby was returning to the scene of the crime!

The sound of a car engine reached their ears. Max grabbed Sid and Zeekie and they melted into the hedge. Holding his breath, Max pushed aside the foliage and saw George stumble out of sight just before Mrs. Clementine's shiny vintage car turned onto the street. Once it was gone, George fought his way out of the bushes, glanced over his shoulder in the direction the car had taken, then disappeared up the driveway.

"We've got to follow him," Max said in a low voice.

"We can't go in there," protested Sid. "That's trespassing!"

"George is the one trespassing," said Max. "We're catching him red-handed. Or green-thumbed."

Sid bit her lip. "I don't know ..."

"He's going back to get rid of the evidence," whispered Max. "Fingerprints or something. We've got to catch him in the act!"

"I'll stand guard," offered Zeekie. His eyes were round with excitement. "If anybody comes, I'll give the signal."

"Good," said Max. "Are you coming, Sid?"

"Maybe I should stay out here with Zeekie," Sid said.

"Sure," said Zeekie. "Can I hold the walkie-talkie? We need secret code names like truckers use on their CBs, only they don't call them code names, they call them handles. You can be Skippy Dippy and I'll be Captain Boomerang. Or maybe ..."

Sid hurried after Max. "Wait for me!"

15 Oopsy-Daisy

Max and Sid tiptoed toward Mrs. Clementine's house, placing their feet carefully so that they didn't make any noise. Ahead of them, George was far less careful. Twigs snapped under his feet, and he stumbled twice before he reached the door.

"What's he doing?" whispered Sid.

George rattled the door handle. It didn't open. Furtively, George glanced over one shoulder, then the other.

Max and Sid darted behind a bush. A floppy pink bloom brushed Sid's nose and her nostrils quivered.

"Don't sneeze," mouthed Max. He wished he had some broccoli. Or horseradish.

Sid rubbed her nose and slowly exhaled. They turned back to George, who was picking through the rocks in the flowerbed beside the front door.

"He's going to break in," breathed Sid.

Max nodded. "I'll bet he's going to smash the glass in the front door!"

They watched as George chose a fist-sized rock.

Sid's right nostril twitched.

George hoisted the rock from one hand to the other.

Sid's left nostril twitched.

George stepped closer to the door.

Both of Sid's nostrils twitched. Her eyes watered. Max thrust his finger under her nose, but it was too late.

"Ahhh ... ahhhh ... *CHOOOOO!*"

George froze. "Who's there?"

Sid's nose twitched again. Max gulped. Another sneeze! He pinched her nostrils shut and held on for dear life.

"AAAHHH ... AHHHH ... *CHOOOO!*" The second sneeze seemed to ricochet around the yard like a bullet.

"Run!" shouted Max.

Everything seemed to happen at once. George lunged toward the bush where Max and Sid were hiding. Max tried to yank Sid to safety, but she couldn't run and sneeze at the same time.

And a strange humming filled the air.

Max flinched at the sudden sound of glass shattering. Peeking around the bush, he saw George staring, open-mouthed, at Mrs. Clementine's green-house, and beyond that, a flash of yellow among the grass. Then he heard the frantic *squilch, squilch,*

squilch of flip-flops on gravel.

"I heard the signal!" cried Zeekie. "I heard Sid's signal and I saw that man chasing you. I got him with my boomerang. Sid? Max? Can you hear me?"

"*You* were supposed to give *us* the signal," Max cried. His ears were ringing. "*You're* the lookout, remember?"

Zeekie paused. "Oh yeah. Right." He looked at the greenhouse. Its door was now a crinkly spiderweb of broken glass, like a windshield that had been beaned with a rock. "Oopsy-daisy."

"What in tarnation is going on here?" demanded George.

Max scrambled to his feet, pulling Sid up with him. "We've got to call the police."

Sid pointed at the driveway. "Look! They're already here!"

The ringing in Max's ears blended with the wail of a siren as a police car pulled up, its lights flashing.

Officer Todd stepped out of the patrol car.

"I just got a report of an alarm being tripped," he said. "What's going on?" He surveyed the scene, taking in George, the rock, the boomerang, and the cracked greenhouse door. Then his gaze came to a

85

rest on Max.

"You," he said.

"Hi, Officer Todd," said Max. "Nice to see you again."

Officer Todd said nothing.

Max got right to the point. "Arrest that man!"

"Why?" asked Officer Todd.

"Trespassing," cried Max. "Breaking and entering. Premeditated plant murder!"

"I'm just looking for my glasses," protested George. "I lost them last night when the lights went out."

"Lies!" cried Max. "You were going to smash in the window!"

George flushed. "What? No, no ... I just wanted to get my glasses. That's all."

"You just wanted to get rid of the evidence," corrected Max. "Like fingerprints on a certain thousand-dollar orchid. If people found out that you murdered Victor, it would cost you the Green Thumb election."

Before George could reply, another car pulled up and Mrs. Clementine hurried over. "What happened? I saw the police turn into my driveway ..." She stopped when she saw the greenhouse.

Zeekie edged away from the boomerang and pointed at George. "He murdered Victor," he said helpfully.

Camilla quickly punched some numbers into a keypad mounted near the greenhouse door. The ringing stopped. Then she turned to face them all.

"I want some answers," she demanded. "And they had better be good!"

16 True Confessions

"I didn't touch your orchid," said George. "I'm here for my glasses. I'm as blind as a bat without them."

"He had motive," cried Max. "He hates Mrs. Clementine. He was jealous of her prize-winning orchid! He didn't want people to vote for her for president!"

George looked dazed. "What are you talking about? I don't hate Camilla."

"I knew he still liked her," crowed Sid.

Mrs. Clementine's cheeks grew pink.

"He was going to smash the door with a rock," insisted Max. "He's guilty, I say!"

"You mean this rock?" asked George. He flipped the rock over, revealing a secret compartment. "Camilla used to keep this key hidden for emergencies. Back when we were dating."

George and Camilla looked at each other, blushing.

"But he had means, too," persisted Max. "He was at the meeting. He could have pushed the plant over when the lights were out."

"Actually, half the town was there too," Sid reminded him.

"You really don't hate me?" Mrs. Clementine asked George.

George cleared his throat, embarrassed. "Nah. I've always admired your spunk."

"Really? All those wasted years ..." said Mrs. Clementine, her fingers at her throat.

"Hey, folks," said Max, glancing at Sid, whose eyes were suspiciously misty. "I think we're getting off topic here ..."

"Shush," whispered Sid. "You'll spoil the moment."

"I swear I didn't ruin your orchid," George added. "But I will admit I was jealous. Anyone can grow a big old pumpkin. You deserve to be president, not me."

"Hello?" Max looked around helplessly. "Victor's dead, remember? Murdered? Isn't that a federal offence or something?"

"I don't know about that," said Officer Todd. "But we'll need to fill out a damage report for the broken greenhouse. I'm sorry, George, but you're going to have to come down to the station while we sort this out."

George sighed. "I'm sorry too, Camilla. For everything. Maybe if I hadn't been so stubborn all these years, things could have been different ... "

Officer Todd raised his eyebrows. He and George started toward the police car.

"Wait," cried Mrs. Clementine. "I don't want to press charges."

Officer Todd turned. "Well, actually – "

"None of this is his fault," insisted Mrs. Clementine. "It was all me."

"You?" repeated Max, Sid, and Zeekie at the same time.

A single tear rolled down Mrs. Clementine's cheek. "George is an ornery old coot, but he's not dishonest. I knocked the orchid over myself. Accidentally. Someone jostled my arm, I lost my balance in the dark – it was just a foolish accident. But I let people think it was George so they would vote for me instead. I'm the one who should be arrested."

"This silly rivalry has gone on too long," George said, wiping away her tear with a callused thumb.

"How did you make the lights go out?" asked Zeekie.

"My house is old," said Mrs. Clementine with a faint smile. "Everything in it is old, too. Including the wiring."

George flushed. "You heard that?"

"No matter." Mrs. Clementine sighed deeply. "It's true. I refuse to press charges against George," she told Officer Todd. Bravely, she held out her wrists. "Take me instead."

Sid gasped.

Officer Todd looked uncomfortable. "I wasn't actually arresting him, there are just a few forms to fill out ... routine stuff, really ..."

"I lied," cried Mrs. Clementine. "I slandered George's good name. I tried to influence the voters. Take me to jail – *I* deserve to be punished, not George."

George gazed at Camilla. "You'd do that for me?"

Camilla smiled. "Yes. For old times' sake. We

used to be such good friends, remember?"

George took her hand. "Like it was yesterday. To be honest, I can't remember why we fought."

"Me neither," said Camilla, smiling sadly.

A small sigh escaped Sid's lips.

"I guess we could run as co-presidents," suggested George, bringing her hand to his lips. "I guess I could help fix your greenhouse. And help you grow another orchid."

"I guess that means no reward money," said Max glumly.

Sid threw her hands up in disgust. "I don't believe you, Max! When are you going to learn that not everything is about money?"

Max's shoulders slumped. "Maybe you're right."

The two new lovebirds looked at Max, and then at each other. George dug in his pocket and held out a crumpled paper.

Max looked at it. "Ten percent off your next purchase at Sportz Zone?"

Sid snatched the coupon out of his hands. "*Whoo hoo!* That super-deluxe catcher's mitt is all mine!"

Max snorted with disgust. George and Camilla were too busy holding hands and gazing into each other's eyes to notice.

"Come on, kids," said Officer Todd. "I'll give you a ride home. It looks like these two have some catching up to do."

"Cool!" cried Zeekie. "I've never ridden in a police car before. Can I put on the lights? And the siren? Can I use the radio? Do you have a computer in there? What about – "

"Well, Max," said Sid as she settled into the

back seat of the cruiser. "It's back to the flowerbox business for us, right?"

Max sighed. He wasn't so sure. He'd done some mental calculations. Once they bought Mom a new watering can and paid for Mrs. Clementine's broken flower vases and greenhouse door, he figured that by the end of the summer they'd have made a whopping profit of exactly three dollars and seventeen cents.

"You think anyone would be interested in one slightly used gardening business?" he asked.

Zeekie stopped pestering Officer Todd. "Are you serious?" he asked Max.

Max shrugged. "Sometimes you just have to cut your losses."

"Can I take over Go 'n' Grow?" asked Zeekie. "Please, please, please? I'll pay everyone back for the stuff I boomeranged and I'll take super-good care of the flowers for the whole summer and I'll spray the bugs and scoop the poop and ..."

"A corporate takeover?" Max paused, then stuck out his hand. "That's the best idea I've heard all week. You've got yourself a deal."

Zeekie let out a whoop of joy and turned back to Officer Todd. Max slouched down in his seat and sighed. "At least *he's* happy."

"Look on the bright side," Sid said with a laugh. "You patched up a life-long rivalry. And brought two lonely people together. You can't put a price on true love."

"Yeah, I guess they looked pretty happy too," agreed Max. His brain began to buzz. Maybe Sid was right. Maybe he did have a special knack for bringing people together. He could open his own dating service. Build a web site. People would send him videos from all across the country, looking for love. Maybe he'd even get his own television show ...

"Max the matchmaker," he said, grinning at Sid. "I think I like the sound of that!"

About the author:

Trina Wiebe received her first typewriter when she was eight years old and has been writing stories ever since. She is also the author of the "**Abby & Tess Pet-Sitters**" series (Lobster Press), which *Quill & Quire* says is "reminiscent of Beverly Cleary's Beezus and Ramona." She lives in Invermere, British Columbia.

About the illustrator:

David Okum is a high school art teacher and author who lives in Waterloo, Ontario. He wrote and illustrated *Manga Madness* (Impact Books), and his artwork can be found in several manga anthologies and small press comic books.